FARMER'S GARDEN

Rhymes for Two Voices

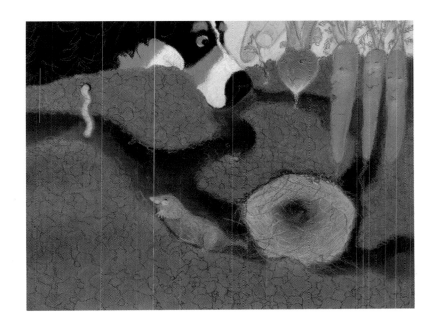

by David L. Harrison

Illustrated by Arden Johnson-Petrov

Wordsong
Boyds Mills Press

Redbird

Redbird, Redbird,
why do you sing?

> *I sing for joy!*
> *It's spring!*
> *It's spring!*

Do you have babies
in your nest?

> *Yes! And we don't*
> *get much rest.*

Where have you
hidden your nest so well?

> *In Farmer's garden,*
> *but I can't tell!*

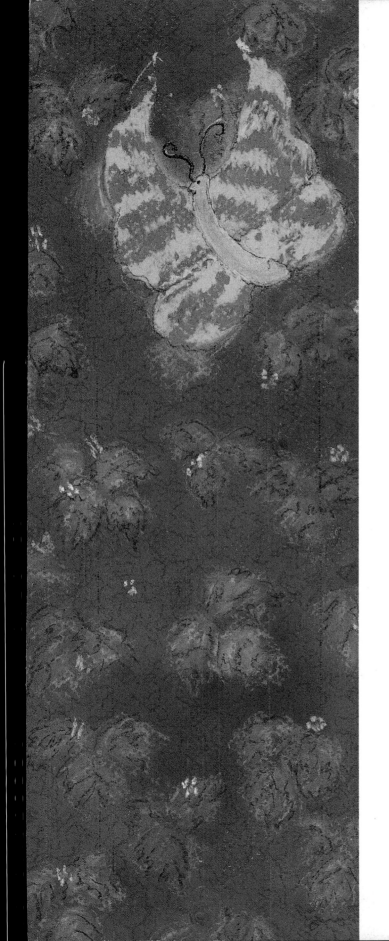

Butterfly

Butterfly, Butterfly,
where have you been?

Out to the garden
and back again.

Butterfly, Butterfly,
what did you see?

A hungry spider
smiling back at me.

Butterfly, Butterfly,
what did you do?

I fluttered my wings
and away I flew!

Strawberry

Strawberry, Strawberry,
juicy and red,
how do you like the garden?

> *Life is good*
> *in the strawberry bed,*
> *sunning in the garden.*

What if Farmer
thinks you're sweet
and plucks you from his
garden?

> *Strawberries dream*
> *of being a treat*
> *plucked from Farmer's garden.*

Mousey

Mousey, Mousey,
why do you hurry?

Cat is coming!
I must scurry!

Cat is coming?
Hide! Hide!

His teeth are sharp!
His mouth is wide!

Where will you go?
You can't get far.

Then I will hide
in Farmer's garden.

Bunny

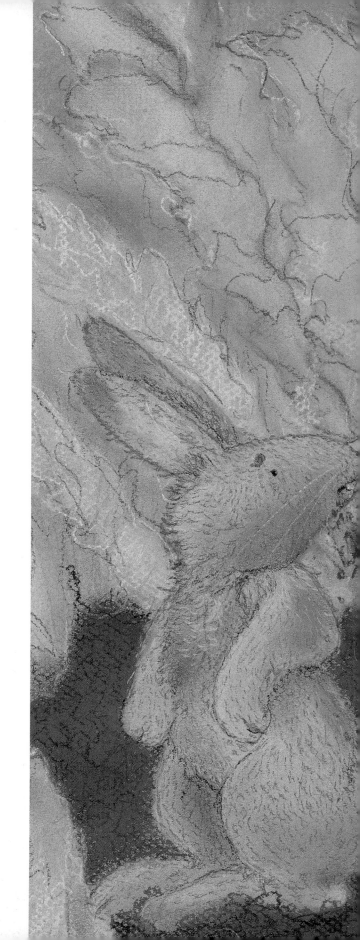

Bunny, Bunny,
what do you do?

*I nibble and chew,
nibble and chew.*

What if Farmer
shakes his hoe?

*I hippity-hop
and off I go!*

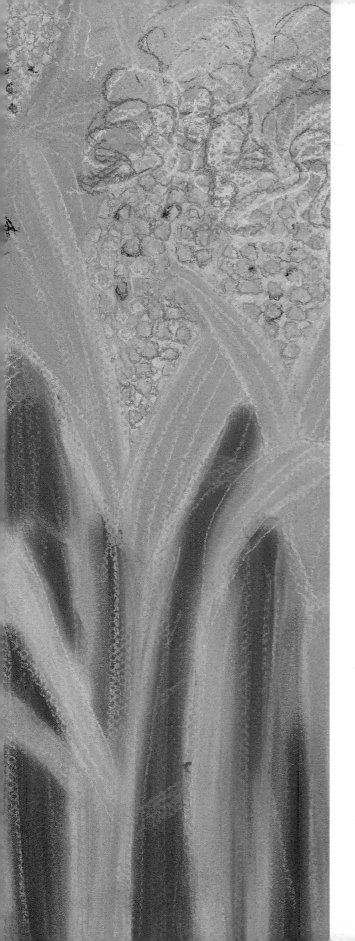

Corn

Corn, Corn,
how do you grow?

Tall and straight,
row on row.

What do you do
when Crow flies near?

Hope he doesn't
nibble my ear!

What do you do
when he flies away?

Have myself
a mighty fine day.

Cow

Cow, Cow,
why did you do it?
Why did you trample
the garden?

> *The gate was loose*
> *so I came through it,*
> *chewing and trampling*
> *the garden.*

Shoo, Cow!
Be on your way!
You'd better get out
of the garden!

> *I'll go to the barn*
> *and chew some hay*
> *and* moooove *on out*
> *of the garden.*

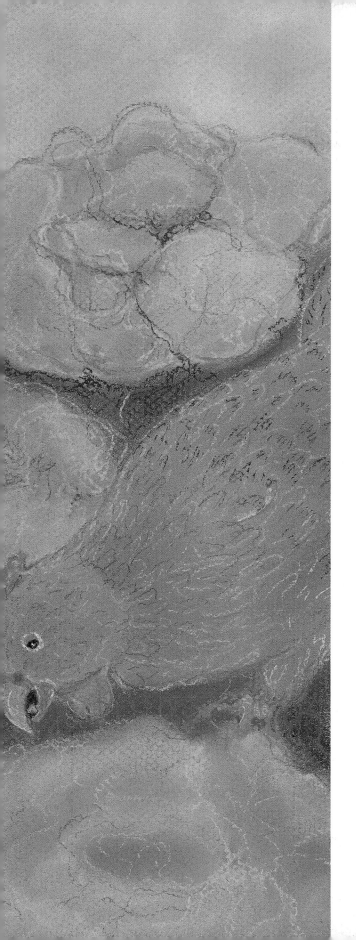

Chicken

Chicken, Chicken,
what do you find
scratching in the garden?

*Yummy seeds
of every kind.
Mmm! I love the garden!*

Is it wise
to scratch up dirt
inside the Farmer's garden?

*What can it hurt
to scratch up dirt?
I like it in the garden.*

Chicken, Chicken,
what's your plan
if you're found
in Farmer's garden?

*I'll squawk as loud
as a chicken can
and run outside the garden.*

Worm

Worm, Worm,
what do you eat?

> *Delicious dirt*
> *is such a treat!*

Why do you wiggle
and squiggle and squirm?

> *It's ticklish business*
> *being a worm.*

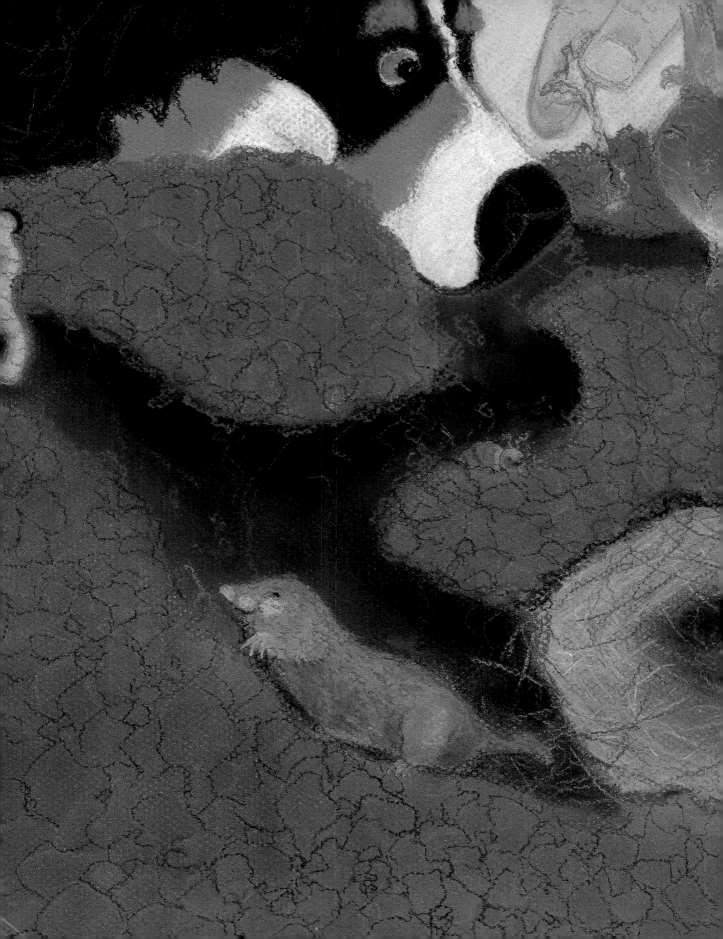

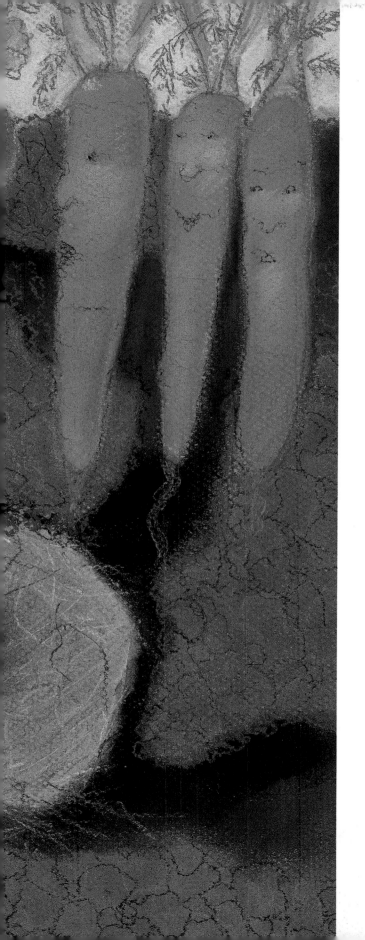

Carrot

Carrot, Carrot,
what do you see
under Farmer's garden?

*Moles and grubs
and roots of a tree
under Farmer's garden.*

Carrot, Carrot,
how can you be
happy under his garden?

*I love it when Farmer
waters me
and weeds me
in his garden.*

Beetle

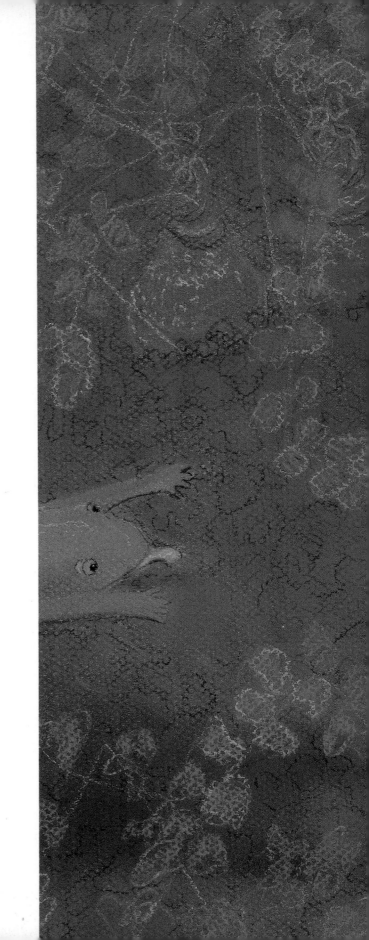

Beetle, Beetle,
why so fast?

> *Out of my way!*
> *I must get past!*

Beetle, Beetle,
where do you run?

> *Away from Lizard*
> *and out of the sun.*

Beetle, Beetle,
what will you do?

> *I'll drink a drop*
> *of morning dew.*

Lizard

Lizard, Lizard,
what do you eat
in Farmer's lovely garden?

*Beetles and bugs
are hard to beat
in Farmer's lovely garden.*

What if Hawk
should spot you here,
sunning in the garden?

*Lickety-split
I'll disappear
until he leaves the garden!*

Radish

Radish, Radish,
reddish and hot,
how do you like the garden?

> *Life is good*
> *in my little plot*
> *tucked in Farmer's garden.*

Radish, Radish,
what will you do
when he picks you
from the garden?

> *I hope to go*
> *in a pot of stew*
> *with all my friends*
> *from the garden.*

Deer

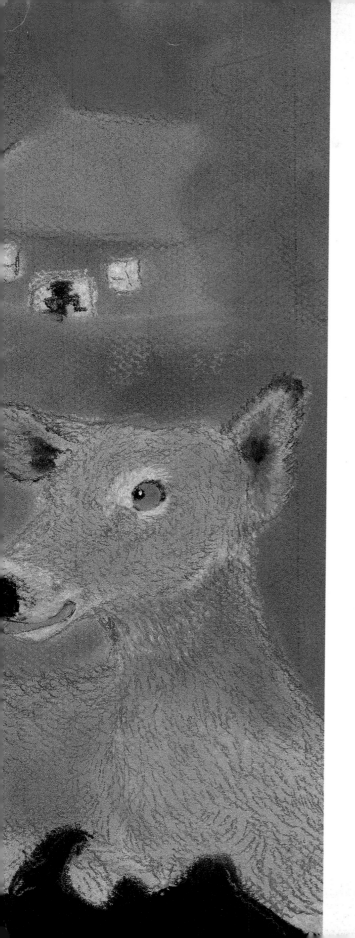

Deer, Deer,
why are you here
tonight in Farmer's garden?

*Shhh! Don't tell him
there's a deer
visiting in his garden!*

Is it safe
for you to snack
by moonlight in the garden?

*Shhh! I'm going,
but I'll be back.
I dearly love his garden!*

Farmer, Farmer,
what do you see?

By the light of the moon,
my dog and me.